ISBN 0-590-25084-1

12 11 10 9 8 7 6 5 4 3 2 1   5 6 7 8 9/9 0/0

Printed in the U.S.A.   23

First Scholastic printing, September 1995

"Hyde and Go Shriek" and "Hunted"

Based on episodes of
Tales from the Cryptkeeper™

Adapted by Jane B. Mason

Illustrated by Erik Doescher

SCHOLASTIC INC.
NEW YORK   TORONTO   LONDON   AUCKLAND   SYDNEY

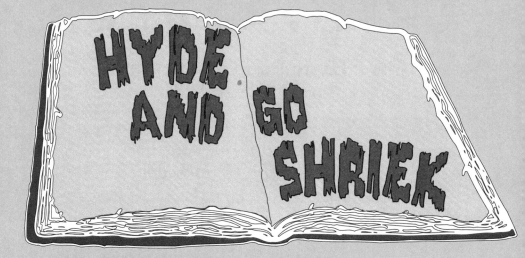

HYDE AND GO SHRIEK

Greetings, fitness fans!

To get your day off to a <u>screaming</u> start, just take a little wheat <u>germ</u>, throw in some gar-<u>bones</u>-o beans, a dash of car-<u>rot</u> juice, and voilà. It's a crypt cocktail—a smooth and creamy <u>chiller</u>. Uh-oh, I guess you'll have to settle for our story. It's about a weakling named Wendell who had a <u>bully</u> of a time until he learned how to play . . . "Hyde and Go Shriek!"

It was gym class at school, and Rex and his buddies were playing a game of football.

"What's my job, Rex?" a guy named Wendell asked. Wendell was a science nerd, but he liked to hang out with the guys, too.

"You play left out, Wendell," Rex said in a mean voice. "Get it? *Left out!*"

Wendell cheerfully headed for the sidelines and got ready for the play. When Rex fumbled the ball a few seconds later, Wendell grabbed it. "What do I do?" he called to his teammates. A bunch of guys from the other team were stampeding right toward him!

Two seconds later, Wendell got tackled—hard. Rex and his buddies, Louie and Chet, howled with laughter. Wendell was such a dweeb!

The three guys were still laughing as they headed into the locker room to change. "That's the best one yet, Rex!" Chet said, opening his locker.

Wendell wasn't far behind. "Yeah, you sure got me that time, Rex," he said good-naturedly.

"You gotta hand it to Wendo, Rex," Louie said. "He can handle whatever you dish out."

"We'll see about that," Rex replied with a smirk.

The guys watched as Wendell opened his locker—all his clothes had been tied into knots. Rex grinned fiercely. "Watcha got there, Wheeze, a tie-dye project for art class?" he teased.

But all Wendell said was, "Gee, what am I going to wear now?"

Rex's grin turned into a scowl. "I'll wipe that grin off his face once and for all if it kills me," he declared.

☙ ☙ ☙

Later that day, Wendell was in the biology lab with his pet rat. "And to think you used to be scrawny like me, Dr. Jekyll," he told it affectionately.

"Lookit the size of that sucker," a voice said.

Wendell looked up to see Rex standing over him. "Dr. Jekyll's my best friend," said Wendell.

Rex reached into the cage and grabbed the rat by the tail. "Is he a pack rat, or a *back* rat?" Rex asked. He dropped Dr. Jekyll into Wendell's T-shirt.

"Whoa!" Wendell exclaimed. He tripped and fell, and Dr. Jekyll tore out of his pant leg. He dashed up the wall and into an air duct.

As the rat disappeared, Wendell let out a cry of anguish. He stood up and turned toward Rex. "This time you've gone too far, Rex," Wendell shouted. "I'm gonna make you pay!"

A few days later, Chet and Louie ran into Wendell in the weight room.

"Need some help, Wendo?" Louie asked as Wendell struggled with a barbell.

"No, thanks," Wendell replied. "I have to do this myself. I'm getting ready to have it out with Rex once and for all."

A mischievous look came over Chet's face. "Listen, you're going about this all wrong," he said.

"Yeah, at this rate you'll be an old man by the time you're ready to take on Rex," Louie agreed.

"You need *immediate* results," Chet told Wendell. "A special program that will build

muscles upon muscles in days."

Wendell's eyes widened. "You guys know where I can get something like that?"

Chet smirked at Louie and the two of them took Wendell across town to Chet's dad's health food store. In the back room, Chet climbed up onto a ladder and pulled down a dusty tin box of tea.

"This'll do—I mean, this is the stuff," he declared. "Guaranteed to turn even the scrawniest dweeb into a bloodthirsty beast overnight."

Wendell's eyes widened. "Wow," he said. "I'll take some."

Wendell paid for the tea and left, leaving Chet and Louie laughing. It was so easy to put one over on old Wendo!

＊　＊　＊

That night, something strange happened. Something scary. A werewolf-like monster was seen prowling through the city streets. It scared the dickens out of two stray dogs. It attacked a man at a newspaper stand. And it crumpled a car like a soda can.

＊　＊　＊

The next morning, Chet picked up a newspaper and read the headlines: "'Monster on the Loose!'" No, it couldn't be?! he said to himself.

"Louie!" he exclaimed. "Maybe the tea we gave to Wendell worked!"

Louie shook his head. "No way," he said.

Chet's eyes were wide. "But if it did work, then Rex is in big trouble. We've got to warn him!"

But Rex didn't believe what Chet and Louie told him. In fact, he decided it was time to *really* teach Wendell a lesson.

"But, Rex, if it *is* Wendell, he's probably waiting out there to get you!" Chet pleaded.

"Good!" Rex answered. "'Cause I've been waiting for an excuse to squish him like a bug!"

That night, Rex walked down a deserted street. As he turned a corner, he heard a voice calling to him.

"I've been looking for you, Rex," Wendell said. He held a thermos of tea in his hands. "It's time you paid for what you did to Dr. Jekyll."

"Yeah, Chet and Louie told me all about your magic tea," said Rex.

Wendell gulped down the hot beverage. A second later, fur began to grow on his neck and face. His nose twisted into a hairy snout. Fangs sprang out from his gums. And long, sharp claws stretched off the tips of his fingers. In seconds, Wendell had turned into a savage beast!

"Gaaaaaa!" Rex screamed in terror and took off down the street. He ran in and out of buildings, but he couldn't escape the Beast Boy. Wherever Rex went, the Beast Boy followed, snarling and snapping at his heels.

After a long chase, the Beast Boy closed in. But just then a police car turned into

the alley. In an instant, the Beast Boy disappeared.

Rex tried to tell the police about the monster, but they didn't believe him.

"Everyone in town's seein' monsters," an officer told him. "We've got every available man on the job. So go home, lock your door, and leave it to us."

🪲   🪲   🪲

Rex knew he had to do something. He couldn't let Wendell get the best of him, even if he *was* a monster. So the next day he found Chet and Louie and they all went to the health food store.

"This is it, Rex," Chet said, handing him the box of tea.

"Better not be holding out on me!" Rex warned.

"It's the whole box. Honest. All we got!" replied Louie nervously.

Rex made a strong pot of tea and gulped it down. A few minutes later he was transformed into a hairy, muzzled monster, even bigger and scarier than the Beast Boy!

For a second, Chet and Louie could only stare in horror. Then they bolted out of the store, running for their lives.

The monster chased after them, but as soon as he got out the door, ten police cars pulled up.

"Rrrraarggruh?!" said the confused Rex Beast.

"There it is. Fire the tranquilizer," ordered the policeman in charge.

The Rex Beast flinched as the dart hit him. A second later he fell to the ground with a thud.

Louie and Chet watched from behind a building. "You know," said Chet, "I get the feeling Wendo knew that this was the way it was going to go down...."

🪲　　🪲　　🪲

"Monster Identified as Local Youth" read the newspaper headlines the next day. Everyone in school was talking about Rex the Monster.

Wendell grinned knowingly as he opened his locker door. A small, furry rodent was sitting on his books.

"Dr. Jekyll, you came back!" Wendell exclaimed. He scooped up the rat and set him on his shoulder.

Just then, Chet and Louie came around the corner. When they saw Wendell, they froze in their tracks.

"Woof," Wendell said in his geeky voice. Chet and Louie jumped and raced back down the hallway. They knew who the real monster was—Wendell.

Hello, <u>boils</u> and <u>ghouls</u>,

As you can see, I'm taking this terror tale on the road. It's a blood-chilling tale about an <u>inhumane</u> <u>hunter</u> who could <u>scare</u> less about the animals he trapped! But little did he know he was about to get caught up in his own wicked ways. I call it . . . "Hunted."

Ahunter walked slowly through the jungle. It was hot, and the jungle leaves were thick, but the hunter had been hired to bring rare animals back to the United States. It would make him rich.

Suddenly, a jaguar appeared, and the hunter stumbled backwards in fear. But just as the jaguar sprang toward him, a net swept it off the ground. The animal snarled and growled furiously, but it was trapped.

A group of natives—including a young boy—watched the hunter fire a tranquilizer dart at the big cat. A second later, the cat was asleep.

Later that day, everyone was back at camp.

"You people should have led me this far into the jungle before," the hunter said to the boy as he greedily eyed the many animals he had caught and caged.

The kid smiled. "I've read about zoos," he replied. "The animals will be well cared for there, right?"

The hunter shook his head. "Those animals are going to end up as everything from fur coats to rugs to fancy appetizers," he said with a mean laugh.

The boy's eyes widened in concern, but the hunter didn't seem to care. "Let's just keep this conversation between you and me," he said. Then he walked off.

That night at dinner, the hunter noticed that the native men were talking loudly together.

"You didn't tell them about our conversation this afternoon, did ya?" he asked the boy.

The boy shook his head and eyed the darkness anxiously.

"Come on, kid. They're worried about something," said the hunter.

"We have come too far," the boy answered solemnly. "Our legends tell of a devil beast that can change shape like a ghost! It is called Onnaya."

"That's a bunch of baloney!" the hunter declared.

But later that night, something strange happened.

Suddenly, the constant jungle noises—growls and chirps and buzzes—stopped. A great silence filled the air. Then a huge black shadow crept into camp. The caged animals shrieked and growled. And when the hunter and the boy ran to the cages, all of the animals were gone.

The hunter was furious. "Whatever that was, it robbed me blind!" he shouted. He turned toward the natives. "And nobody saw anything?" he asked in disbelief.

"We *heard*," the boy said.

"Oh, right," the hunter sneered. "The silence."

The boy didn't say anything. Instead, he pointed to a footprint on the ground. It was huge—two feet long—and had five webbed toes. Next to the print was a patch of long, thick black fur.

The hunter bent down and picked up the fur. "I've never seen fur like this," he said. His eyes lit up with greed. If he could catch this rare animal, he could get really rich! "Whatever it is, I'll bet there's only one of 'em. We're talking big bucks for this baby!" exclaimed the hunter.

But the boy's eyes were fearful. "Onnaya," he said.

The hunter licked his lips eagerly. "Tell them to break camp," he told the boy. "We're going after it."

But the natives were huddled together in a group, whispering. They looked afraid.

"It is no use," the boy said. "They will not go."

"I need someone!" the hunter exclaimed desperately. "I'll pay you double. Triple!"

The boy bit his lip, thinking. Finally, he nodded. "Okay," he said.

The next morning, the hunter and the boy slowly made their way through the jungle. It was hot and muggy, and the thick vines and plants made it difficult to walk. After a while the hunter stopped for a drink, but his canteen was empty. And when he looked up, the boy was gone!

"Kid!" he shouted. "Kid!" But only the birds and monkeys answered.

Just then, the hunter heard a noise right behind him. He spun around nervously...and saw the boy. He was holding a piece of fruit and grinning from ear to ear.

The hunter scowled, but the boy explained that the fruit would quench his thirst. He took the fruit and greedily began to eat.

While the hunter slurped, a snake began to slither up his boot. He pinned it against the ground with his rifle. Then he realized he'd only pinned the tail. The snake was at least twenty feet long, and it was hissing like crazy! The boy and the hunter rolled to safety just in time.

Later on, the two came to a swampy part of the jungle.

When the hunter stepped on to a mostly submerged log, he heard a low growl. The log was really a crocodile with a giant mouth full of sharp teeth!

The croc charged at him while the boy scrambled to safety. Then, just as the giant croc was about to attack the hunter, it turned and swam away. "Why do you think it did that?" the hunter asked, gasping.

The boy looked around nervously. "I can guess. We should turn back," he replied.

"Why? What is it?" the hunter asked. "Not your ghost?"

Just then the jungle became deathly quiet. A second later, a loud thrashing sound echoed through the air. Then the boy and the hunter saw a huge, dark shape tear by them through the thick jungle foliage. Onnaya!

The boy leaped to his feet and started to head back the way they came.

"Wait! You can't leave me, kid!" the hunter yelled.

"If you do not come with me," the boy said, "the legends say that Onnaya will swallow your spirit!"

"But we had a deal!" the hunter exclaimed. But the boy was already gone. He would have to track the beast by himself.

The hunter moved forward through the jungle. The foliage was even thicker than before, and he had to struggle with every step. But he told himself it was worth it. The beast would bring in a lot of money.

The hunter pushed aside a jungle bush and saw a small rise of dry land in the distance. He made his way toward it and threw himself onto the ground.

And then it happened—the jungle grew completely silent.

The hunter lifted his head as a big, dark shape moved toward him. The beast!

It stepped into view, and the hunter gasped in horror. Its arms were long and thick, with five-toed claws at the ends. Its eyes were cold and wolf-like. And its crooked mouth gaped open, showing rows of yellow fangs!

The beast let out a fierce bellow. Then it turned and ran farther into the jungle.

The hunter was on his feet in a second. He chased after the beast. "Yaargh!" he cried, charging through the thick growth. After a while he found the beast squatting in the middle of a clearing.

The hunter moved forward, pointing his tranquilizer gun at the beast. "At last!" he bellowed. "The hunted has finally given up! The hunter has won!" he grinned. "You don't know what I've gone through to get you!"

But as he spoke, a net rose up under his feet, yanking him into the air. "Yaahh!" he cried, alarmed.

"And you wouldn't believe what I went through to get *you* here," the beast replied.

Stunned, the hunter stared at the beast. "You were hunting *me*?" he asked.

The beast nodded. He told the hunter that he was once a hunter for hire, too. He'd searched for the rarest of animals— those that would bring in the most money.

Suddenly, the hunter noticed that the escaped animals he had hunted were coming out of the forest and sitting in a circle around his net. He began to tremble in fear.

"One night I was badly injured by a rare white panther," the beast said. "A magician saved my life. But he cursed me as well."

At that moment, the animals and the beast looked up at the bright moonlight. And before the hunter's eyes, the beast began to change!

His arms and shoulders lost their fur and their weird shape. His large, floppy ears melted away. And his fangs disappeared. The beast was becoming a man!

As the hunter stared in shock, his body changed, too. His neck disappeared. His teeth turned into horrible fangs. His fingers were replaced by sharp claws. And thick, black fur grew on his skin. He was becoming the beast!

"The curse can never be removed," the man who had been the beast said. "Only passed on." He looked directly at the beast in the net. "You have become the very beast you hunted!"

The new beast whimpered, but there
was nothing he could do. He was no longer

The old beast turned and walked away, and the animals went their separate ways, too. And in another part of the jungle, a native boy caught up to his tribesmen. They exchanged a knowing look, then moved off through the thick foliage. As he pushed a giant leaf aside, the boy looked over his shoulder. "Onnaya!" he said.

Don't Miss...
Tales from the Cryptkeeper #1